Meow!
Will you answer the call for adventure?

Kitty

and the
Sky Garden Adventure

Greenwillow Books
An Imprint of HarperCollinsPublishers

For Emmeline. Welcome, little bean.–P. H.

For Mum and her green thumb–J. L.

Kitty and the Sky Garden Adventure
Text copyright © 2019 by Paula Harrison. Illustrations copyright © 2019 by Jenny Løvlie
First published in the United Kingdom in 2019 by Oxford University Press; first published in hardcover and paperback in the United States by Greenwillow Books, 2020

www.harpercollinschildrens.com. The text of this book is set in Berling LT Std.

Library of Congress Cataloging-in-Publication Data

Names: Harrison, Paula, author. | Løvlie, Jenny, illustrator.
Title: Kitty and the sky garden adventure / written by Paula Harrison ; illustrated by Jenny Løvlie.
Description: First edition. | New York : Greenwillow Books, an Imprint of HarperCollins Publishers, 2020. | Audience: Ages 4–8 | Audience: Grades K–1 | Summary: Kitty and her feline friends discover a secret roof garden and learn all about plants and gardening.
Identifiers: LCCN 2019041824 | ISBN 9780062935489 (paperback) | ISBN 9780062935496 (hardcover)
Subjects: CYAC: Superheroes—Fiction. | Human-animal Communication—Fiction. | Gardens—Fiction. | Cats—Fiction.
Classification: LCC PZ7.H256138 Kiv 2020 | DDC [Fic]—dc23
LC record available at https://lccn.loc.gov/2019041824
20 21 22 23 24 PC/LSCC 10 9 8 7 6 5 4 3 2 1
First Edition

Greenwillow Books

Contents

Meet Kitty & Her Cat Crew

Kitty

Kitty has special powers—but is she ready to be a superhero just like her mom?

Luckily, Kitty's cat crew has faith in her and shows Kitty the hero that lies within.

Pumpkin

A stray ginger kitten who is utterly devoted to Kitty.

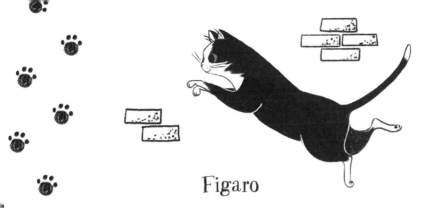

Figaro

Wise and kind, Figaro knows the neighborhood like the back of his paw.

Pixie

Pixie has a nose for trouble and whiskers for mischief!

Katsumi

Sleek and sophisticated, Katsumi is quick to call Kitty at the first sign of trouble.

Chapter 1

"Look at this, Pumpkin. My sunflower's starting to grow!" Kitty gazed at the small plant in its little brown pot. She was sitting on the flat rooftop above her bedroom while the stars appeared one by one in the evening sky.

"It's got two leaves already!" said Pumpkin, a roly-poly ginger kitten with big blue eyes.

Kitty touched the sunflower's sturdy stem and pointy leaves. "I'm definitely putting sunflowers into my design for the new school garden. I just wish I had a few more ideas. . . ."

She frowned thoughtfully.

Kitty had been delighted when her teacher had told the whole class about the competition to design the new school garden. All they had to do was draw their plan for the garden on a piece of paper and color it in carefully.

Her teacher had also said they could try growing a plant for the garden right away. Kitty had chosen a sunflower because she loved their beautiful round faces and flamelike petals. Kitty gazed at the sunflower and tried to imagine a new school garden. It was hard to know where to begin.

Darkness had
fallen and a bright full moon
hung in the sky, pouring silvery
light over the houses. The streetlamps
of Hallam City winked below them
and in the distance an
owl hooted.

Kitty loved being out in the moonlight. She had special catlike superpowers, so she could easily climb and balance on the rooftops. Her night vision let her see in the dark, and her super hearing picked up sounds from a long way away. She felt at home up here, and when the moon came out, the world became shiny and magical. She loved sharing this special world with Pumpkin, the ginger kitten she'd rescued from the clock tower many weeks ago.

Kitty leaned in to look more closely at the sunflower plant. The night wind blew gently across the rooftop, making the plant's leaves flutter. There was the soft sound of paws padding over the roof. Kitty listened carefully. "Pixie, is that you?"

"You guessed right!" A fluffy white cat with green eyes sprang out from behind a chimney. Her pale fur gleamed in the moonlight. "How did you know it was me?"

"I used my super hearing. Your paw steps sound lighter than Figaro's and quicker than Katsumi's or Cleo's." Kitty smiled. She had lots of good friends among the cats of Hallam City, and meeting up with them on the rooftops was one of her favorite things to do.

"Hello, Pixie!" Pumpkin scampered

up to the white cat and they touched noses. "Have you come to play with us?"

"Yes, I was looking for something to do," admitted Pixie. "I felt like having an adventure, and I thought to myself: who would be the best person to have an adventure with? Kitty, of course!"

Kitty laughed. "That's very kind of you! I'm just trying to decide what to put in my design for the new school garden. I'd love to win the competition, but I'm not sure what to draw."

Pixie blinked thoughtfully and swished her snowy tail. "I've heard of a place across the city with an amazing rooftop garden. Hardy anyone knows about it, and no one ever goes there because the old cat who guards the rooftop is so fierce. Maybe we could creep up to take a look. It might give you some ideas for designing your school garden."

"But what if the old cat catches us?" Pumpkin's whiskers quivered.

"We'll have to be quiet and sneaky. That's what makes it an adventure!" Pixie jumped onto the chimney, her green eyes glittering with excitement. "It's not far away, so we could get there in a whisker!"

"I'd love to see this garden!" Kitty glanced down at her clothes. "But I'm not really dressed for an adventure. Just one second!"

She darted down the sloping roof and slipped through her bedroom window. Taking her black superhero suit from the closet, she quickly pulled it on. Then she added her velvety cat ears and tied the dark, silky cape around her neck.

The moonlight poured over Kitty as she climbed across the windowsill. She felt her superpowers grow stronger, and her body tingled from her head down to her toes. Her eyesight became clearer and her hearing sharpened. Climbing to the top of the roof, she smiled at Pixie and Pumpkin. "I'm ready now—let's go!"

They ran along the rooftop together. Kitty beamed as she jumped from one building to the next, her black cape flying out behind her. She loved the feel of the night breeze on her face and the way the moonlight shimmered on the windows.

The breeze grew stronger, rocking the trees in the park as they passed by. Pixie led them past Kitty's school, with its square playground and jungle gym. Kitty spotted her own desk and chair through the classroom window. A pile of neatly sharpened pencils lay on the teacher's desk, ready for the next day.

On the street behind the school, there was a building site for a row of new houses. At the corner of the site, the builders had left a large bin full of odds and ends they were throwing away.

Every now and then Pixie stopped to sniff the air. "Yes, it's this way," she called to the others. "I can smell the scent of flowers."

Kitty smiled. "I can smell them, too!" The sweet scent drifting on the night breeze reminded her of roses.

One by one they jumped from the rooftop to the ledge of an apartment building. Then Pixie led them up the steps of the fire escape. The scent of flowers grew stronger, and Kitty's heart skipped. She raced ahead and climbed onto the wide, flat rooftop. Her stomach fizzed with excitement as she gazed all around.

Trees and flowers filled every corner, like a fountain of bright colors. A winding path made from round, white stepping-stones curved through the flower borders. A group of silver birch trees lined the entrance, making an archway of delicate white branches. Kitty beamed. She'd never seen such a beautiful garden growing on a rooftop before.

Pumpkin and Pixie sprang onto the roof beside Kitty. Pumpkin stopped with a gasp, his blue eyes as wide as tennis balls.

Pixie ran straight under the

archway of silver birches, mewing excitedly. "I'm so glad we found it! This place is amazing."

"It's wonderful!" Kitty stepped under the archway of trees. Gazing upward, she saw the stars sparkling brightly through the web of branches and leaves. She walked on, and a cluster of tall, bright sunflowers caught her eye. She stopped beside the towering plants. "Look at these sunflowers! They're the biggest ones I've ever seen."

There were seven sunflowers altogether, each one taller than Kitty, and they nodded their heads gently in the breeze. She gazed at them admiringly, and their cheerful faces seemed to smile down at her.

She reached up to touch the nearest flower. The golden petals were silky smooth around the rough, black center.

Kitty tingled with excitement. There was something special about this garden. The plants were so perfect, they looked as if they were grown with magic!

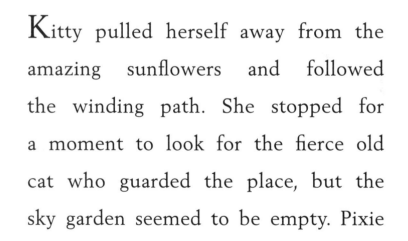

Chapter 2

Kitty pulled herself away from the amazing sunflowers and followed the winding path. She stopped for a moment to look for the fierce old cat who guarded the place, but the sky garden seemed to be empty. Pixie scampered after her, swishing her tail with excitement.

Pumpkin hid behind the sunflowers. "Are you sure we're safe?"

"I don't think anyone else is here," said Kitty. "Come and look, Pumpkin. This place is lovely!"

"It's more than lovely," mewed Pixie. "It's magnificent! And it smells like heaven."

Kitty passed a yellow rosebush growing beside a pink rosebush. She leaned in to sniff them. "These roses smell

wonderful. Which ones
do you like best?"

Pixie and Pumpkin didn't reply, so Kitty turned around to look for them. The little white cat and the ginger kitten were taking turns leaping into the middle of a purple-flowered bush and rolling from side to side with their paws in the air.

"What are you doing?" cried Kitty. "This isn't our garden!"

"It's a catnip plant, Kitty," giggled Pixie. "I just can't help it!"

"Whee!" said Pumpkin, jumping into the bush and rolling around again.

Kitty hurried across to the catnip bush. She'd heard of a plant that cats loved, but she hadn't realized it could make them act so silly. "Stop, Pumpkin! Stop it, Pixie!" she told her friends. "What if the owner of the garden comes along?"

"What's going on here?" said a deep voice. "None of you should be in this garden. Don't you know you're trespassing?"

Kitty's tummy lurched guiltily. Turning around, she spotted a huge shadow with pointy ears on the wall.

She gulped. Was it the fierce old cat who guarded the rooftop? Pumpkin squeaked with fright and hid behind Kitty's legs.

"I'm extremely disappointed that you came in without even asking," growled the voice.

"You're right—we should have asked! We heard how lovely the garden was, and we wanted to see the place for ourselves." Kitty peered through the cluster of plants.

There was the sound of paws padding through the undergrowth, and an old tortoiseshell cat with gray whiskers appeared. He twitched his ears disapprovingly. Pixie leaped out of the catnip bush and began grooming her tail, pretending that she'd been behaving sensibly all along.

"I was having a lovely quiet evening before you all turned up," grumbled the tortoiseshell cat.

"I'm sorry—we didn't mean to disturb you," said Kitty. "My name's Kitty, and this is Pixie and

Pumpkin." The tortoiseshell cat was still frowning, so Kitty continued hurriedly. "Do you live here with your owner?"

"That's right." The tortoiseshell studied each of them suspiciously. "I'm Diggory, and my human, Mrs. Lovett, created this whole place. She's spent years getting it perfect, so I won't let you young rascals come along and ruin it all!"

"We only came to take a peek at the place. You see, I've got to draw a design for a new school garden," explained Kitty. "I'm sorry my friends were so silly when they smelled the catnip plant."

"We're *really* sorry!" Pixie blurted out.

Pumpkin hung his head and stared at the ground.

"Well, I suppose the catnip plant *is* quite exciting," Diggory said slowly. "It does make us silly—like humans when they eat too many sweets. I'm a bit too old to roll around in it these days, though."

Kitty smiled. The old cat was gruff at first, but he wasn't as fierce as Pixie had described. "So do you think we could look around for a little longer?" she asked shyly. "We'll be careful around the plants, I promise. It's just such an amazing place—I would love to see the rest of it."

"We're not really accustomed to having visitors. It can get a little lonely at times, and it's hard to manage looking after the garden with just the two of us," Diggory told them. "It would be nice to share the place with someone

who is interested in the plants." He
turned slowly and led them down
the stepping-stones.

"Thanks!" Kitty followed the tortoiseshell cat eagerly. They passed under a trellis covered with tendrils of sweet-smelling honeysuckle. A tiger moth fluttered under the archway, its orange-and-black wings flickering like a flame. Diggory stopped beside a beautiful bench decorated with carved wooden leaves. He waved a paw at a cluster of white star-shaped flowers growing beside it. They glowed brightly like tiny lights. "These spring stars are Mrs. Lovett's favorite flowers. They remind her of how much she likes to sit here and look at the stars from time to time."

"What a lovely name!" Kitty looked up in surprise as music tinkled in the tree above her head. Hanging from a branch was a wind chime made from delicate seashells. The breeze ruffled the tree, making the wind chime sway. Musical notes drifted over the garden like a magic spell, and the flowers seemed to lean toward the enchanting sound. Kitty's skin prickled as she listened, watching the dangling chime twist and turn. The shells' pearly sheen gleamed in the moonlight.

Diggory noticed Kitty's gaze. "It's beautiful, isn't it? That wind chime is Mrs. Lovett's pride and joy. She made it herself from seashells she gathered as a little girl. I don't think the garden would be the same without it."

Pixie leaped up the tree to the branch holding the wind chime to take a closer look. "It's so pretty," she mewed. "Don't you think it's shiny, Kitty?" She padded closer, and the branch began to bend under her weight.

"Yes, I do . . . but I think you'd better get down!" Kitty quickly climbed onto the bench and steadied the branch with her hand.

Pixie turned around and darted back down the tree trunk. Diggory frowned as the wind chime jangled alarmingly. Kitty let go once the branch was steady. Then she sat down on the wooden bench and gazed at the amazing plants all around her. Pumpkin leaped onto the bench beside her, yawning, and curled up with his furry head in her lap.

"There's so much to see!" Pixie scampered up and down the winding path. "I don't think I could ever get bored here."

"I don't want to go, but I suppose it's getting quite late," said Kitty. "Do you think we could come back tomorrow? I'd really like to get some more ideas for the school competition."

Diggory nodded. "I'd

forgotten how nice it is to show visitors around. You're welcome to come back, Kitty. I will watch for you."

"Thank you!" Kitty smiled at the tortoiseshell cat. "See you tomorrow."

Pixie, Pumpkin, and Kitty made their way back through the archway of silver birch trees. Kitty took one final look at the sky garden before climbing onto the fire escape. The night breeze swept across the garden, rustling the leaves and making the sunflowers nod their heads.

The wind chime
twisted and turned, winking
in the moonlight and playing its
beautiful music. The magical sound
echoed around Kitty's head as she
darted across the city rooftops
and home to bed.

Chapter 3

The next evening, there was a tapping on Kitty's bedroom window just after moonrise. Kitty opened the window and smiled. "Hello, Pixie! You're quite early tonight."

"I love being early!" Pixie leaped

into the room, her green eyes gleaming. "Shall we go back to the sky garden now? Wouldn't you like to get some more ideas for your design?"

"Yes, I would! It's such a beautiful place." Kitty turned to Pumpkin, who was lying on the bed with his stripy tail wrapped around his ginger tummy. "Are you ready to go, Pumpkin?"

Pumpkin stretched his paws and yawned. "I'm ready. I was just having a quick catnap!"

Kitty put on her

cat superhero costume. Then she and Pixie climbed out the window and up to the rooftop. The breeze ruffled Kitty's hair and made her cape swirl around her legs. Stars began appearing one by one like tiny sparks in the darkening sky. Pumpkin climbed after Pixie and Kitty, still yawning.

Pixie ran to the edge of the roof and sniffed the air eagerly. "Come on—let's not waste any time!"

Kitty jumped to the next building, her cape flying out behind her. Pumpkin and

Pixie padded after her. They ran along the rooftops and gazed down at the quiet streets below. When they passed the building site, Kitty spotted a pile of empty paint cans lying inside the trash bin. The metal cans glinted as the moon came out from behind a cloud.

Pixie streaked ahead, reaching the apartment building with the fire escape.

"Slow down, Pixie," called Kitty, laughing. "You're as fast as a cheetah tonight!"

"I can't help it!" Pixie's words floated

back to her. "I'm too excited to go any slower."

Kitty stopped suddenly, her hand on the rail of the fire escape. There was a lot of mewing and yowling coming from the rooftop. She had been too busy talking to Pixie and Pumpkin to notice it before.

"Kitty, do you hear that?" Pumpkin shrank back. "Maybe we shouldn't go up there."

An earsplitting screech cut through the night, followed by a burst of wild laughter.

A cold prickle ran down Kitty's neck. "That sounds like it's coming from the sky garden!" She darted up the metal steps, trying to catch up to Pixie.

The little white cat hesitated at the

edge of the rooftop. Her snowy tail
flicked to and fro and she pinned her
ears back in alarm.

"Pixie, what's wrong?" Kitty raced up the last few steps. Her heart sank as she reached the top and stared around the crowded garden.

There were cats everywhere—black ones, white ones, ginger, gray, and tabby. They were dashing along the paths, trampling over the flower beds, and pouncing on one another in the bushes. Three cats were climbing the archway of silver birch trees, and several delicate white branches had already snapped off and fallen to the ground.

Diggory, the old tortoiseshell cat, was pacing up and down, shaking his head. His fur stood on end and his gray whiskers were shaking. "Get down from there!" he mewed at one of the cats in the trees. "Get your paws off that rosebush!" he snapped at another.

Pixie's tail swished nervously. She gazed around with wide, shocked eyes.

"Diggory, what's happening?" cried Kitty. "Where did all these cats come from?"

"I don't know. They've been arriving

for hours, and they won't leave!" growled Diggory. "They've torn down the lights on the honeysuckle trellis and trodden on so many beautiful flowers. I knew it was a mistake to let visitors in here! When Mrs. Lovett sees the garden, she'll be heartbroken."

"But why are they here? I thought people didn't really visit the garden." Kitty noticed Pixie's ears were drooping. The little cat looked terribly guilty. "Pixie, did you tell lots of cats about this place?"

Pixie nodded with a wailing meow. "I'm *really* sorry! I was just so excited after seeing this place that I told everyone how amazing it was and I said the cat who lived here wasn't scary at all! I didn't think they'd all rush over and ruin the garden."

Diggory shook his head sadly. "What am I supposed to do? These cats won't listen to me. Most of them have rolled in the catnip plant, and nothing I say will stop their ridiculous behavior!"

"We're so sorry, Diggory!" said Kitty,

giving Pixie a stern look. "We'll get these cats to leave before things get any worse. Pixie, you guard the catnip plant and don't let any cats touch it. Pumpkin and I will round them up and send them home."

Kitty rushed over to a group of cats climbing on the garden bench. She took a deep breath, saying firmly, "It's time to go! And don't come back again unless Diggory invites you."

A small tortoiseshell cat tried to hide behind the honeysuckle vines.

"You're just a bossy boots!" she shouted as Kitty shooed her out of her hiding place.

"Be careful! That's the owner's favorite flower," Pumpkin cried as a black cat trampled right through the spring stars bush.

A plump cat with thick gray fur and droopy whiskers was perched halfway up the wind chime tree. "Ooh, look! It's the Garden Police! Why are you making such a fuss? We're only having a bit of fun." He fixed Kitty with his cold blue eyes and flexed his sharp claws. The tree branch rocked and the wind chime jangled.

"Your *fun* is ruining the garden!" said Kitty. "And please don't damage that wind chime. It's very precious!"

The plump cat eyed the wind chime.

Then he yawned, showing off his pointed teeth. "You can't keep a special place like this all for yourself. It's very selfish!" He began grooming his long fur.

"Hey, Duke!" yelled a small tortoiseshell cat. "Come and try out this catnip plant."

The plump gray cat waved at the other cat before turning back to Kitty. "Don't you think you should learn to share a little? If you don't, you might be very, *very* sorry!"

Kitty frowned. "Why? What do you

mean . . ." She broke off and ran to help Pixie, who was struggling to keep cats away from the catnip plant. "You'd better leave quickly," she told them. "If the owner comes out, you'll be in a lot of trouble."

"Well, the fun is *clearly* over!" Duke climbed down from the wind chime tree and shook his long whiskers angrily. He glared at Kitty again before heading to the edge of the rooftop. When he snapped his claws, the other cats slunk after him, mumbling complaints.

"It's not fair!" cried the tortoiseshell cat. "We were having a nice time before you came along."

Kitty shook her head at the creature's rudeness. The cats crowded toward the fire escape, yelling at one another and trampling on the flower beds. At last they were gone.

A lump rose in Kitty's throat as she gazed around the sky garden. The place had looked so perfect yesterday evening. Crushed petals and torn leaves were scattered across the stepping-stones. The earth was covered with paw marks, and snapped branches lay on the ground.

Pumpkin looked up at Kitty with anxious blue eyes. "What are we going to do?"

Kitty looked across at Diggory. The old cat was trying to straighten the bent branches of the spring stars bush.

A large tear rolled down his furry face.

Kitty swallowed. "We're going to fix this! If we work hard as a team, we can put the garden back together again."

Chapter 4

Kitty dusted off her hands. "We must fix this before morning! We can't let Mrs. Lovett wake up and see the garden looking this way."

Diggory shook his head. "There's no need to do anything! I know you're only trying to help, but Mrs. Lovett and I always look after this garden by ourselves."

Kitty crouched down beside Diggory. Her heart sank as she saw how tired and sad he looked. "Please let us help! I promise we won't stop until the garden looks better again."

"We could start by cleaning up the broken

flowers and leaves," suggested Pumpkin.

Diggory frowned. "Well, all right, then. I'll show you where the broom is." He led them to a small brown shed in the corner of the rooftop.

Kitty took out a rake, a broom, and some gardening gloves. She swept along the stepping-stones, while Pixie and Pumpkin picked up the broken flower stems and dropped them into the compost bin. They raced up and down the garden. Kitty's heart thumped. They had to hurry if they were going to finish cleaning up before sunrise!

Pixie and Pumpkin began tidying the fallen leaves. Kitty snipped some drooping stems off the rosebush and tied the honeysuckle back onto the trellis. She watered each sunflower, as their leaves were drooping. One flower was broken beyond repair, but the others soon seemed much better again.

"What shall we do about all these, Kitty?" Pumpkin pointed to a row of smashed flowerpots with dirt spilling out the sides. The purple lavender growing in each one had a strong, sweet smell.

"We don't have any spare pots, I'm afraid." Diggory shook his head. "We'll have to throw away that lavender."

A determined look shined in Kitty's eyes. "These flowers are much too pretty to lose! We'll just have to find a few pots somewhere." She darted to the metal stairs, calling to Diggory, "Don't

worry—we'll be back soon!"

Pumpkin scampered after Kitty, with Pixie close behind.

"Where are we going?" Pixie waved her fluffy, white tail. "None of the stores will be open, Kitty. We can't buy new flowerpots till tomorrow morning."

"I know—but that'll be too late!" Kitty rubbed her forehead worriedly. "Maybe there's something else we can use. Let's look around and see." She leaped to the roof next door before clambering down a drainpipe. Crossing the road carefully, she stopped beside a row of newly built houses.

Kitty spotted a pile of empty paint cans at the top of the builder's rubbish bin. An idea popped into her head. She took out the paint cans and checked each one. "These are clean and they're just the right size! I think they'll look lovely with flowers inside."

"That's a great idea!" mewed Pumpkin.

Pixie leaped onto the side of the bin. "How about this bucket? And look—here is a pair of red rain boots. Wouldn't they look nice with plants growing in them?"

"They'd look wonderful!" Kitty beamed. "All kinds of recycled things

will work as flowerpots." She gathered up the bucket and the old boots and carried them back to the rooftop. Then she returned to fetch the empty paint cans.

Working as fast as she could, Kitty filled each container with soil. Then one by one, she planted the flowers inside them. Lavender bloomed from the paint cans, and yellow tulips sprouted from the old red boots. A silver-winged moth fluttered through the air and rested on a tulip, flexing its delicate wings.

Kitty finished sweeping before climbing the trellis to hang the lights back in place. Then she raked the flower bed to get rid of all the paw prints. Pumpkin and Pixie tidied more fallen leaves from the stepping-stones. Kitty's heart skipped as she gazed around. They'd finished repairing the garden before sunrise!

Pixie and Pumpkin sat on the bench for a rest while Kitty went to find Diggory. The old tortoiseshell cat was sitting beside a stone basin filled with water, gazing at the moon's reflection in the rippled surface. He looked at Kitty mournfully. "I guess sweeping and tidying can't really make up for all the damage that was done."

"No, but we replaced the broken pots and replanted all the flowers. Come and see!" Kitty nervously led Diggory toward the center of the garden. The recycled

flowerpots they had chosen were very different from the ones that had been used before. She really hoped the old cat would like them!

Diggory followed Kitty around the garden. He listened carefully while she explained about reusing the paint cans and the old red rain boots. Slowly, a warm smile grew on his face and his ears pricked up.

"So we hope you like what we've done," said Kitty shyly. "We can change things back again if you don't."

"No, you don't need to do that!" Diggory told her. "I wouldn't have thought of it myself, but these recycled pots look wonderful."

"That was all Kitty's idea!" Pumpkin said.

Kitty brushed dirt off her hands. She couldn't shake the feeling that something wasn't right. The garden didn't feel as magical somehow. The flowers didn't lean toward the center of the garden the way they had before.

Diggory tottered toward the garden seat. A gust of wind swirled over the rooftop, rocking the tree behind the bench. Diggory stiffened and peered closely at the long branches. "Nooo!" he yowled. "It's gone! The beautiful wind chime is missing."

Kitty gasped, staring at the empty branch. Where had the wind chime gone?

"Wait! Maybe it just fell to the ground." Pixie jumped down from the bench to search.

Pumpkin joined her, and they all

hunted through the bushes. Kitty climbed the tree to check that the wind chime wasn't hanging on another branch, hidden by the leaves.

"One of those naughty cats must have taken it," said Kitty at last.

"Maybe we can make a new one by reusing old things like we did with the flowerpots," said Pumpkin hopefully.

"That just won't do!" mewed Diggory. "It isn't just any old wind chime. Mrs Lovett made it from seashells that she gathered as a child. All the love and care that went into making the wind chime turned it into something magical. I don't think the garden will grow the same without it."

Kitty gazed around the sky garden. The flowers had lost their bright sheen, and the trees rattled in the wind. Even the sunflowers bowed their heads sadly. The magic of the garden had vanished, like a cloud hiding the moon.

"This is my fault!" Pixie's voice trembled. "I was the one who told all those careless cats about the garden."

"I'll use my super hearing to find them," said Kitty. "They can't have gone very far."

"Please be careful," said Diggory. "Goodness knows what those wild cats will do next!"

"Don't worry!" said Kitty. "We've faced tricky adventures before. We'll search the city until we get the wind chime back again!"

Chapter 5

Kitty ran from one corner of the roof to the next. She listened desperately for the tinkling sound of the wind chime. At first all she could hear was the wind whistling around the chimney. Then her super hearing grew stronger, and she caught a faint jingling noise.

"Pixie! Pumpkin! I think I can hear it." Kitty raced over the rooftops. She sprang from one roof to another, turning a somersault as she leaped over a chimney.

As she ran, she strained to hear the distant sound of the wind chime. Sliding down a drainpipe, Kitty followed the sound to an alleyway between two tall houses.

She crept to the edge of the roof and crouched beside the gutter. Turning to

Pixie and Pumpkin, she put a finger to her lips.

A group of cats had gathered in the alley below. Kitty recognized many of them from earlier that evening. The group was crowding

around Duke, the plump cat with the droopy whiskers, as he held the wind chime up in the air. The silvery seashells glinted in the moonlight.

"Now, listen!" Duke shook the wind chime roughly. "I've had enough of your yowling."

"But Duke!" whined a tall ginger cat. "I was the one who sneaked that dangly thing out of the garden, so I should get to keep it."

"It should be mine! I carried it all the way down the drainpipe," complained a black cat. "You would have lost it somewhere."

"No, I wouldn't have!" said the ginger cat crossly.

More cats joined in, all mewing and complaining at the same time.

"*Enough!*" yelled Duke. "If you can't agree, then we'll break the chime and each take one piece."

Kitty gasped. How dare he think of taking apart the magical wind chime? Without it, the sky garden would never be the same again. She couldn't let that happen!

"What should we do, Kitty?" whispered Pumpkin.

"Leave it to me!" Kitty whispered back. "I'm going down there."

Duke began pulling the seashells off the string and throwing them to the other cats.

Kitty's heart thumped as she looked at the alley below. The ground was a long way away, but her superpowers would help her.

She balanced on the edge of the rooftop, spreading her cape with her

hands. Taking a brave leap, she plunged
through the air. "Cat power!" she yelled
as her cape flew out, slowing her fall.

She landed lightly in front of Duke,

steadying herself with one hand on the alley wall.

"Look, everyone!" said Duke with a sneer as he pulled more shells off the wind chime. "It's the silly girl who chased us out of the sky garden."

"Give those shells

back!" cried Kitty. "The garden won't be the same without the wind chime."

"Tough luck!" Duke laughed nastily and threw a shell to a black cat. "Here— catch, Howl."

"Stop it!" Kitty leaped into the air, reaching as high as she could, but the shell sailed over her head.

Duke laughed even harder and threw more shells through the air. Kitty caught one, but she missed the next and chased after the tall ginger cat, who scampered away down the alley.

"We'll help you, Kitty!" Pixie clambered down the drainpipe, followed by Pumpkin.

Kitty, Pixie, and Pumpkin chased after the cats. Kitty dashed to and fro, turning head over heels to catch the silvery shells. Soon she had a handful tucked in her pocket, but Duke was still pulling more of them off the wind chime.

"There are too many cats and too many shells, Kitty!" panted Pumpkin.

Kitty paused to catch her breath. Tears came to her eyes as she saw the empty strings dangling from the wind chime. There was no more beautiful sound, only the noise of the wind in the alley and Duke's laughter.

"You thought you could beat us, didn't you?" crowed Duke. "But you're not fast enough to catch us all!"

Kitty gazed despairingly at the cat gang spread out

along the alley. Suddenly she noticed a few of them shaking their seashells and frowning. Another cat was tapping his shell against the alley wall.

"It's not working!" complained the tall ginger cat.

"Stupid shell!" said the black cat. "What happened to the tinkly noise?"

Kitty shook her head. "The wind chime only makes a sound when the pieces are joined together," she explained. "Shaking one on its own doesn't work! We have to put all the shells back on the string again."

The cats looked at one another uncertainly.

"Don't pay any attention to her!" growled Duke, but Kitty wasn't finished. She saw that she had their attention and leaped up onto a trash can so all the cats could see her. She had to make them understand!

"Listen, I know you were really cross when I told you all to leave the garden," she continued. "I am not a bossy boots, and you were wrong to mess around in the trees and the flower beds . . . but maybe we should have found a way to enjoy the place together."

Some of the cats murmured and nodded.

Pixie's ears pricked up, and she whispered, "Keep going, Kitty! I think they are finally listening."

"Why don't you all go back there with me?" suggested Kitty. "If you each say sorry to Diggory, the owner's cat, and give back your piece of the wind chime, then I'll talk to him about letting you visit."

"That's a stupid idea!" scoffed Duke.

"You'll have us singing songs to the moon next!"

The group of cats gathered together, whispering and meowing.

"Hey!" Duke's whiskers quivered. "You're not actually *falling* for this, are you?"

At last, a thin tabby cat with a crooked ear padded up to Kitty. "We'll come with you and take the shells back to where they belong."

"That's awesome!" Kitty beamed and shook the tabby's paw. "My name's Kitty.

Anyone else who wants to do the right thing and return the wind chime should follow me. If we're quick, we can get back to the sky garden before sunrise."

A line of cats followed Kitty down the alley and then onto the rooftop. Duke yelled up at them as they trooped around the chimneys. "You're all being stupid! Cats are meant to be wild and naughty. Cats are meant to do whatever they like!"

"Be quiet, Duke!" the tabby called down. "You're just upset because we're not doing what *you* want anymore."

When Kitty reached the sky garden rooftop, she held up her hand to signal the cats to wait. Hurrying down the stepping-stones, she found Diggory alone on the bench, staring sadly at the stars.

"Those cats have come to apologize for all the trouble they caused," she told Diggory.

The old cat scowled. "After all they've done, I'm surprised they dared to show their faces!"

"I know they were really naughty, but they say they're sorry now. Wouldn't it be nice to have visitors in the garden sometimes?"

Kitty noticed Diggory's tail twitch thoughtfully. "They have all the shells for the wind chime, so if you have some spare string, we can put the chime back together again," she said.

Diggory's ears pricked up. "There's some string in the shed. I'll fetch it right now!"

Chapter 6

Kitty brought the cats onto the rooftop, and they lined up along the stepping-stones. Looking around at the sky garden, they began whispering to one another and pointing to the flowers and the new flowerpots.

"Did you do all this, Kitty?" asked the tall ginger cat. "It looks so tidy."

"My friends Pixie and Pumpkin helped too," replied Kitty.

Diggory returned with some thick green string, and the tabby cat with the crooked ear stepped forward with a shell, looking very ashamed of herself. "I'm truly sorry for wrecking your garden," she mewed. "I was horrible and selfish, and I promise I'll never do anything like it again."

Diggory nodded. Taking the shell,

he threaded it onto the first piece of string. After that each cat came up to apologize and to add their shell to the string. Soon there were five long threads full of beautiful silvery shells.

When Diggory had finished arranging the shells, worry creased his whiskery face. "Kitty, we're missing the piece in the middle that makes it chime."

"Duke has that piece. I bet he will be here any minute now." Kitty crossed her fingers behind her back. She really hoped she was right, and that Duke would arrive with the missing piece soon!

Diggory sat on the bench, patiently holding the strings of shells. The cats gathered around him, gazing at the seashells as they twisted and turned in the night breeze.

Pixie and Pumpkin ran to the edge of the roof and peered at the street below.

"I can't see anyone," called Pixie, sadly. "No, wait!"

Pumpkin danced around in a circle. "It's Duke! He's climbing up the fire escape."

Kitty held her breath as the plump gray cat clambered onto the rooftop. He stroked his whiskers before clearing his throat. "I'm . . . I'm sorry I caused so much trouble," he said to Diggory, his tail drooping. "Your garden is amazing, and I shouldn't have rushed in and ruined it all."

Diggory frowned before

taking the chime from Duke. "Well, we all make mistakes from time to time," he said slowly. "Perhaps I should have invited visitors here sooner. So if you promise to keep to the paths and look after the plants, then . . . you're welcome to stay."

Duke clapped his paws together with excitement, before catching himself and trying to act cool. "Sure—I can promise all that! It looks nice now that the place is neat again."

Diggory carefully tied the chime

between the strings of shells. Then
Kitty climbed the tree behind the
bench and hung the chime carefully
from a long branch. Everyone watched
and waited.

There was a moment of silence.
Then a breath of wind swirled over

the rooftop, making the seashells sway.
The wind chime tinkled softly, and all
the cats cheered.

Diggory smiled widely. "This has
been a night of surprises. Thank you,
Kitty, for making me realize how much
I've missed having visitors." He climbed
down from the bench. "Now I'd better
water the plants like I do every evening."

"Why don't you sit and rest? We can
finish the chores." Duke clapped his
paws. "Everyone fill up the watering
cans!"

Kitty and Diggory sat on the bench together while Duke and the other cats got to work. Pixie scampered up and down the path, telling the other cats all about their garden rescue.

"Do you have any good ideas for your school garden design, Kitty?" said Pumpkin, jumping up beside them on the bench.

Kitty gazed around the sky garden. "I'm definitely going to use recycled flowerpots, and lots and lots of sunflowers!"

Pumpkin snuggled against her. "What a busy night! I'm very sleepy now."

Kitty smiled and yawned. "Me too! But I'm so glad that we had a new adventure and made some wonderful new friends!"

Super Facts About Cats

Super Speed

Have you ever seen a cat make a quick escape from a dog? If so, you know they can move *really* fast—up to thirty miles per hour!

Super Hearing

Cats have an incredible sense of hearing and can swivel their ears to pinpoint even the tiniest of sounds.

Super Reflexes

Have you ever heard the saying "Cats always land on their feet"? People say this because cats have amazing reflexes. If a cat

118

is falling, it can quickly sense how
to move its body into the right position
to land safely.

Super Vision

Cats have amazing nighttime vision. Their
incredible ability to see in low light allows
them to hunt for prey when it's dark outside.

Super Smell

Cats have a very powerful sense of smell.
Did you know that the pattern of ridges on
each cat's nose is as unique as a human's
fingerprints?

Meet Kitty!

Girl by day.

Cat by night. Ready for adventure!

The Kitty books—read them all!

1

Is Kitty brave enough to step out into the darkness for a thrilling moonlight adventure?

2

Can Kitty find the thief who stole the tiger treasure and return the precious statue before sunrise?

3

Will Kitty save the wonderous and secret sky garden before it is destroyed forever?

4

Heroic teamwork and a magical feast bring Kitty and a new friend together!

Meowing Soon!

5 Kitty and the Shimmering Paw

6 Kitty and the Shooting Star